This Little Tiger book belongs to:

_____

_____

_____

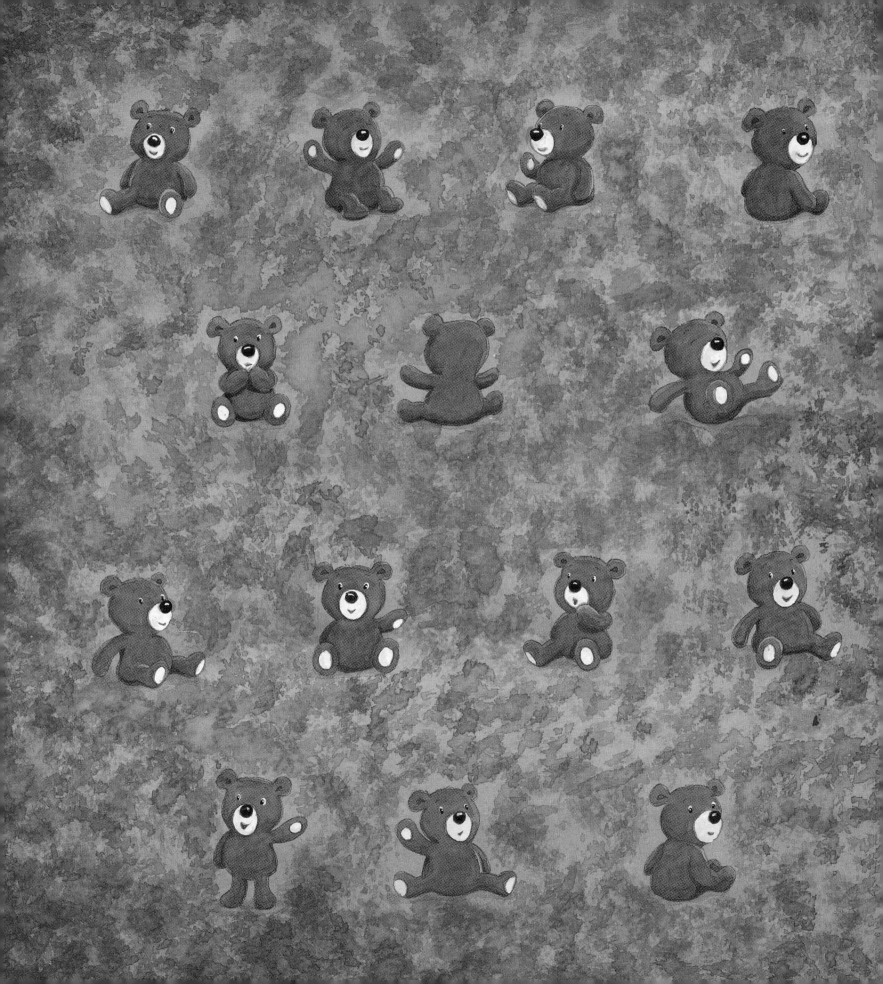

For Mala, whenever you might find things
too big, too deep or too scary . . .

LITTLE TIGER PRESS
An imprint of Magi Publications
1 The Coda Centre, 189 Munster Road, London SW6 6AW
www.littletigerpress.com

First published in Great Britain 2004
This edition published 2004

Printed in Singapore by Tien Wah Press Pte.
A CIP catalogue record for this book
is available from the British Library

2 4 6 8 10 9 7 5 3 1

Come On, Baby Duck!

Nick Ward

Little Tiger Press
London

It was a BIG day for Baby Duck.
A VERY big day!
He was going for his first swim
and he was very excited.

"I can't wait," Baby Duck
said to Teddy. "It's going to
be brilliant. The best day ever!"

"Wait for me!" puffed
Baby Duck, waddling
to catch up with his family.
"Hurry up, slow coach," quacked
his sisters, Minnie and Molly.

"I'm going as fast
as I can. I'm only little!"
"We're nearly there, darling,"
called Mummy Duck.

Splash!

"Look at us," quacked Minnie and Molly.

"Come on, Baby Duck!" said Mummy Duck.

"It's your turn."

Baby Duck stood at the edge of the pond.
"It's very big," he said. "I might get lost."
"Big makes it good for splashing," said Mummy
Duck. "I'll stay close, I love splashing."

Baby Duck looked into the water.
"It looks deep," he said.
"Deep makes it good for diving," smiled
his mummy. "Jump! I'll catch you."

Raindrops started to plop
into the water.
Baby Duck hugged
his teddy.

Splash!

"Jump in, Baby Duck," croaked Little Green Frog. "It's fun!"
Baby Duck dipped his toe into the water. "It's cold!" he shivered. His wings trembled in the wind.

"It's too deep, it's too cold and . . .

". . . it's scary!"

"My little Baby Duck!" said Mummy.
"There's nothing to be afraid of."
She gave him a great big hug.
"Let's just watch the fun for a bit."

The rain pattered down and
the wind started to blow.

Splash!

"Dive in," piped the little fish,
leaping out of the pond.
"You can do it!"

"I can't," whimpered Baby Duck,
 as the wind blew harder.
"It's splashy and horrible!
 I hate it!"

But just then,

who!

The wind blew Baby Duck's
teddy up into the air and . . .

Splash!

"Help!" cried
Baby Duck.
"Teddy can't swim!"

But everyone was too far away. "Hold on, Teddy,"
called Baby Duck. "Here I come!"

Baby Duck jumped.
He dived right in
and he swam
and he swam
and he swam.

"I'm coming, Teddy,
don't worry..."

"You're safe now, Teddy!" said Baby Duck.
"Well done! You did it!" cried his
mummy. "You can swim!"
The sun popped out from behind
the clouds. Baby Duck smiled.

"I wasn't scared," said Baby Duck, hugging his teddy. "I love the water . . . and so does Teddy!

"This is the best day ever!"

Splash!

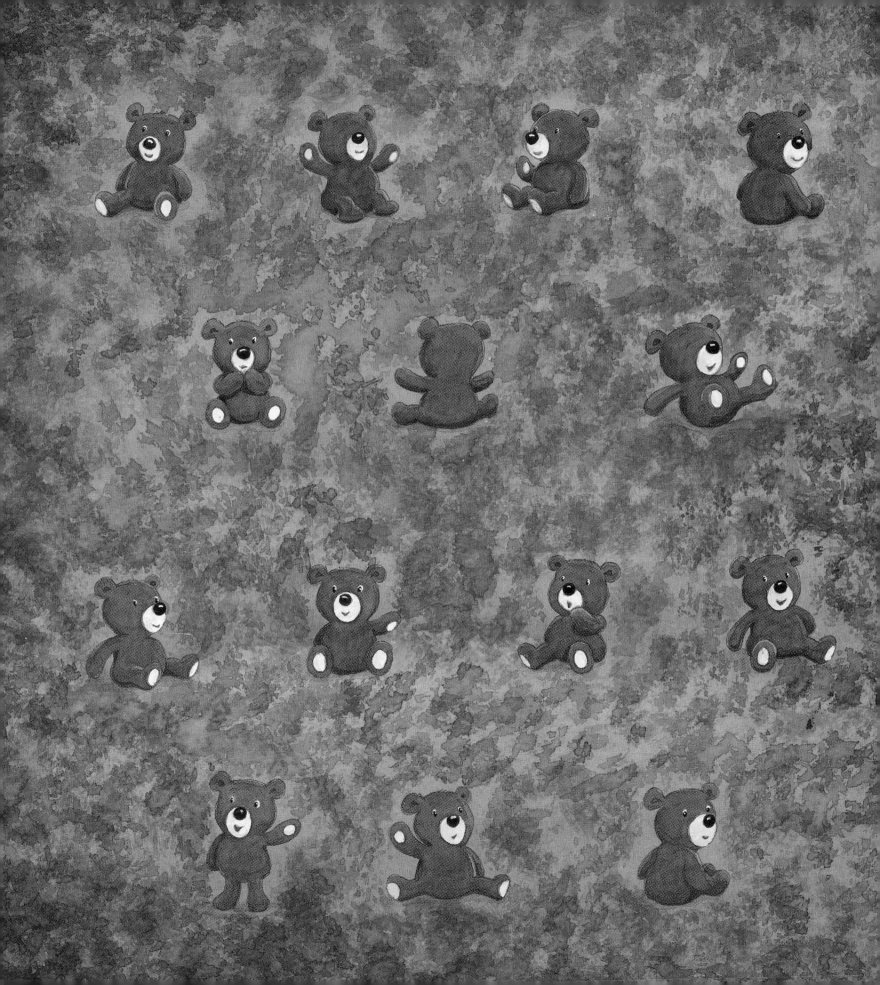

Lots more adventures from Little Tiger Press

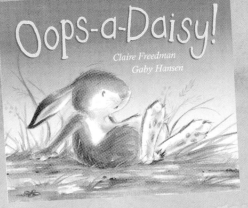

Oops-a-Daisy!
Claire Freedman
Gaby Hansen

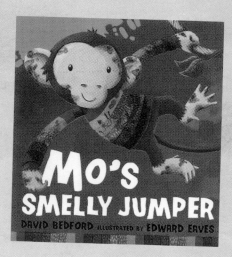

Mo's SMELLY JUMPER
DAVID BEDFORD ILLUSTRATED BY EDWARD EAVES

3, 2, 1 Bedtime
by Sam Lloyd
Illustrated by Ben Cort

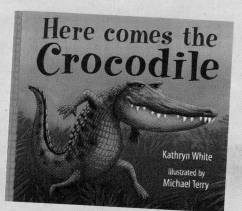

Here comes the Crocodile
Kathryn White
illustrated by
Michael Terry

Where's my Mummy?
Jo Brown

For information regarding any of the above
titles or for our catalogue, please contact us:
Little Tiger Press, 1 The Coda Centre,
189 Munster Road, London SW6 6AW
Tel: 020 7385 6333 • Fax: 020 7385 7333
E-mail: info@littletiger.co.uk
www.littletigerpress.com